The Folger
& Other Lies

Other books by Chris Kelso

NOVELLAS
A Message from the Slave State
Moosejaw Frontier
Transmatic
Rattled by the Rush
Short story collections
Schadenfreude
Terence, Mephisto & Viscera Eyes

NOVELS
The Dissolving Zinc Theatre
The Black Dog Eats the City

ANTHOLOGIES
Caledonia Dreamin'–Strange Fiction of Scottish Descent
(ed. With Hal Duncan)
Terror Scribes
(ed. With Adam Lowe)
This is NOT an Anthology

The Folger Variation
& Other Lies

Chris Kelso

WEIRDO  MAGNET

The Folger Variation & Other Lies
by Chris Kelso

First published in 2016 by
WEIRDO **C** ~MAGNET
an imprint of Leaky Boot Press
http://www.leakyboot.com

ISBN: 978-1-909849-31-0

Contents

Introduction	7
PANCAKE	11
ARTHUR FOLGER	23
EDUARDO	33
THE MURDERER	41
WALKING THROUGH THE FIRE	45
IDLE HANDS	51
THE PROPHET OF TOLERANCE	55
AT 64	59
LAST EXIT TO INTERZONE	73
AFTERWORD	115

INTRODUCTION

Within "The Folger Variation and Other Lies" Chris Kelso provides the authorial version of an Escher painting, one painted on a Möbius strip. Served by plot that loops, twirls, and bifurcates, it is a story to be read in one dedicated burst, and then re-read with a lingering eye and attentive mind.

From the opening, a mental bell rings, and you want to leap from your corner and duke it out with this story. It lunges and jabs at you, always urging you on for more of a beating.

It's a realist voice in an unreal situation. Arthur is the anchor inside this chaotic time stream as he confronts his sins and transgressions alongside that of his mediocre goodness. The consequences bear down on him from every direction.

The imagery helps to drive the story just as much as the disjointed lives of junkie time traveller, Arthur Folger. It's a mystery within a mystery created by the turbulent events caused by the multiple existences of one man.

Kelso draws a taunt line between the real and the imaginary, and then proceeds to tweak it. It's like a chemistry experiment: the individual ingredients poured into a single beaker bubble and spark, reminiscent of the unhinged life of the mad scientist that mixed it. It's the kind of story I used to tear through with excitement in the pages of Heavy Metal.

If Karma and Redemption had a child it would be Kelso's protagonist. We all know Arthur Folger. We've met him and his many faces throughout our lives. Chris Kelso defines Arthur Folger for us, and leads us by the hairs of our nose on his surreal, multi-dimensional journey.

Among a spattering of killer lines, Kelso captures the paranoia and random violence at the edges of cultural assimilation. Arthur holds the unpopular view that the aliens among us are decent folks.

Gio Clairval

I would rather go mad, gone down the dark road to Mexico,
heroin dripping in my veins, eyes and ears full of marijuana, eating
the god Peyote on the floor of a mudhut on the border
or laying in a hotel room over the body of some suffering man or
woman; rather jar my body down the road, crying by a diner in
the Western sun; rather crawl on my naked belly over the tincans
of Cincinnati; rather drag a rotten railroad tie to a Golgotha in
the Rockies;

Allen Ginsberg

PANCAKE

-You got a nice car.

I say this without even thinking. I can't help but marvel at the Roadster and wonder how it fell into the care of such a pretty, but vapid seeming girl. My heart sinks a little when I see the Hello Kitty bobble head she's installed on the dash and the big eyelash decal stuck over the headlight buckets.

I smile at her as I fill up the gas tank. She keeps facing forward, not budging an inch. Planes are rumbling in and out of Los Angeles International Airport filling the air with their jet fume cologne. There was a time when ole' Pancake Patterson could have swept a fine young thing like this off her feet in an instant with his playing alone. I was the great white hope of jazz–but I got an underbite now; brawling in bars has ruined my embouchure, and these days my flesh hangs in a mask of loose, scar tissue over a balding, bovine skull. I'm not in my 20s anymore. No one remembers who I used to be. Christ, *I* barely remember.

I remove the nozzle from the fill cap and pat twice on the storage compartment. The girl speeds away without saying a word.

I was never the most poetic speaker but I could tongue and articulate an alt-sax with smoothness and panache.

It amounts to a hill of beans in the end, of course…

 —— (O) ——

-*SCHUNK!*

The murmuring stops. All I can hear is machinery; the horizontal carousels and automated conveyors that never seem to stop rumbling away in the distance–drums in marching cadence.

-SCHUNK!
I feel another bullet of air disengage from its chamber and thud against my left temple. I can breathe again. Relief washes over me like a glazing of hot honey. I'm always a little surprised by my own relief when the gun doesn't go off. My eyes unclench and take in the warehouse interior, the chaotic jazz of the equipment around me. The flock of factory workers burst into a chorus of cheers and wolf whistles. People are slapping me on the back, tousling my hair. Anything to bring some excitement into their rust-belt lives I suppose. These guys *certainly* don't remember who I used to be. Then again, maybe they do. Maybe that's why it's so damn entertaining. I place the revolver back on the table.
    -BANG!
A celestial face in front of me explodes in slow motion.

The ringmaster twiddles with his anchor moustache, calls into the crowd

–Billy. I say Billy… .

–Yessir?–a black man with eyes like giant squid, a conk haircut and rumpole nose appears.

–Take a seat son. This is yer chance to face off against Ol' Pancake.

Billy drags the chair along the epoxy floor. It screeches but no one winces.

–You know the rules. No palming bullets, no silly faces.

The smell of burnt metal is everywhere. The factory interior is foil silver, an amphetamine users wet dream. I still don't know what they make in this place…

Billy loads a single-round in the revolver, spins the cylinder once and sites the muzzle against his head. Billy's veins are taut bowstrings against dark meat, a veteran of industrial mezzanines. He looks Ol' Pancake right in the eye, communicating a deep calmness that leaves me simultaneously terrified *and* impressed– then proceeds to blow his fucking brains out; ejecting the right hand side of his skull like a jumping jellyfish breaking the water's surface. First shot, what a bummer. Beginners bad luck maybe. Billy's head spins around on its axle a couple of times before he slumps from his chair and wetly hits the factory floor.

A crescendo of cheers erupt and two men come out to drag the limp corpse away to the growing pile.

–NEXT!–the ringmaster screeches coldly.

Another worker, Hispanic-looking and wearing a do-rag around his head, emerges from the sea of faces. His coverall is unzipped at the chest revealing a stained flannel vest beneath. I notice he has cystic acne and ice-pick scars all over his skin, a constellation of herpes blisters on his upper lip. I can't take my eyes from his elaborate corkscrew curls. I can see the fear in his eyes straight away. He'll act cool, but I've seen that look before. All part of the counterphobic attitudes you often see in the eyes of the young, inner-city player. He reaches for the Nagant and his skinny wrists can barely poise the gun. I feel my heart fibrillating. For some reason I don't want this kid to throw his life away.

The klaxon screams above the cheers–lunchtime.

-Saved by the bell–the ringmaster hollers and takes the gun from the Hispanic kid. The sense of liberation in his eyes is incredible. He looks at me all grateful, as if *I* pulled the lunch alarm. Someone stuffs a wad of crushed notes in my hand and pats me on the back.

—— (O) ——

-You seemed scared back there. Were you scared?-I interrupt the silence.

He doesn't say anything.

-If you're afraid of dying why would you come here?

The Hispanic kid lifts his head from the hangdog position and meets my gaze with some reluctance. He answers me with a sad, shamed stare. I recognise this shame.

-Listen, you need money? I haven't got much, but if you promise never to come back to this place I'll give you what I have. I got a mouthpiece given to me by Rahsaan Roland Kirk. It's worth a pretty penny, I'm not all that attached to it either. Just reminds me of someone I used to be but let slip.

The Hispanic kid zips up his boiler suit to fend off the sudden chill blowing in from the city. He doesn't reply, I figure he must be mute or touched in the head. He opens his mouth and air comes out, but no words. Eventually he gets it out. He says

-I loved your stuff Mr Patterson–and walks back in the direction of the factory.

The cold air gets into my bones and the cartilage in my knuckles starts to freeze. I feel a sudden urge to get the fuck out of this industrial estate and back to the outskirts where I belong.

The sun reflects on an inversion layer and I see the hazy vistas of the downtown skyline. A big, ugly red vehicle pulls into the forecourt of the gas station. It's Larry Ferguson from Pasadena. He was once a great drummer himself, no Buddy Rich but he could've been something if he wasn't so dumb and distracted. I guess I'm one to talk.

I make my way to the fuel dispenser, ready to fill his Hummer full of unleaded. Only an idiot like Larry would insist on having a car like a Hummer in this day and age, it gets ridiculously low gas mileage and is slower than a fortnight in the cells. Larry and I are from the same era, when the thick layer of smog hung over LA from all the steel and oil refineries and the old backyard trash incinerators, this was back before catalytic convertors too, of course.

I have a prefrontal headache. I haven't seen him in about 3 weeks, but Larry is hard work and I can't be altogether bothered with his usual bullshit. He leans out the window and nods a hello.

-I'm not ready to start work in the mines. Half my body is paralysed—straight away he's into it. He seems drunk and in no state to drive. Sure enough, the left hand side of his mouth is a little drooped.

-Tell me about it man. We're not getting any younger.

-'How did half my body get paralysed', I hear you ask? Well...

-It's really none of my—

-It's a story that I'm sure you'll find too farfetched to be true, but it is true.

-Ok.

-Some friends and I went up to Arkansas last winter for the guided kayak tours in Cane Creek. We were making our way through the woods to the boat launch cove when I heard strange music coming from a small stone cabin. Imbued with an explorer's curios sprit, which I'd adopted while out on the trail, I went over to investigate. I stuck my head in and saw a bunch of men wearing hazmat suites and playing solitaire.

-Men wearing hazmat suites? No kiddin'.

-I tried to enter the room, but my buddy Miles pulled me out. It was at that moment that half my face became paralyzed. I believe that half my body was caught in some temporal vortex that led to the future.

-And now you're half numb? Maybe it's not a bad thing?

-The left hemisphere of my brain doesn't show signs of normal functioning, it has an abnormal amount of electric waves.

-I can believe that too.

Larry gets out of his Hummer and it makes a noise like an arpeggio rake until he closes the door. He wobbles when his feet touch the ground but he steadies himself against the hood.

I start filling his Hummer. We both gaze at the LA smog. It used to be the smudge pots from the orange groves that were one of the main culprits way back when, now there just seemed to be this lingering atmosphere.

-My son is dead. Buried out at Inglewood cemetery.

-Jesus, Larry. I'm sorry. I didn't know.

-Not many people know. But he's dead.

-Are you ok?

Larry snorts.

-You know, it's funny how your mind works when faced with a tragedy it isn't prepared to deal with. You start thinking about crazy shit, like time travel. I mean, what if I did stumble across a gateway into the future? Maybe there's also a gateway leading into the past, and if there is, would I use it to go back and warn my son that his dealer cut cocaine with rat poison?

-It's natural to think that way, does no good though.

-Hey, don't I know it.

I knew Larry's son. He was a quiet kid who had a job removing plastic flashing with a knife in a factory in Palm Springs. A depressing job for a kid so young. Larry was never much of a father though, I'm sure he'd be the first to admit that.

It isn't like him to be so open. I sense his son's death is weighing heavily on his conscience. If I'm honest I still can't be bothered with Larry's shit.

Mike, the gas station manager, shouts me back over to the point of service. I've never been so grateful to hear his gruff voice yell my name.

-I better take this Larry. I'll talk to you later, maybe I'll see you before you go...

-Sure.

Michael Folger is topless, sweating profusely under the LA humidity. I study the sinews of his back as he reaches behind the counter to retrieve something. When he comes back up he's holding a glassine envelope which he then passes to me.

-A fellah came round this morning, said this was for you.

-Thanks Billy...

He snatches the envelope away from my grasp suddenly.

-I don't care what you get up to after yer shift is done Patterson, but I draw the line at shady characters dropping by to deliver your mail at work.

-I got it Billy. Sorry.

I tear open the seal and unfold a letter inside. It reads simply-ST CHRISTOPHER, SAN PEDRO BAY, 12PM, 2 PRE-LOADED BULLETS, HUNDRED DOLLAR MAX

I re-fold the letter and stuff it in the back pocket of my jeans. Larry gets me thinking about time travel. If it were possible, what would I go back and change? Honestly? Not a goddamned thing.

I arrive early at the harbour. There are sailors coming on and off ships, trawlers loading up, old seadogs loitering who I'd probably see later on at the match. The Port Police are patrolling but rarely ever enter the moored ships. I see a big container ship called *St Christopher*, a massive vessel encrusted with zebra mussels and corroded by salt water along its hull. There's a bearded seaman who waves me aboard. He inhales the smell of the Pacific and leads me onto the ramp. I'm surprised to've been recognised. We silently descend through the ship's decks. He's mumbling to himself.

It's not long before I hear the familiar cheering of the crowd and prickles Ol' Pancake

Patterson's scalp.

I step into the light. The table is centred in the crowd of fifty or so drunken, 'Deer Hunter'-obsessed-seamen. The gun is potted in the middle. I take a seat and the bearded man who led me here comes up and leans on the chair opposite.

-Ok, shut up you animals!

Everyone ceases the din.

-Who's first? Who's gonna take on Pancake himself?

A figure pushes through the sea of bodies and breaks through to the front. It's Larry Ferguson. His eye are set in sunken gutters of insomnia. I saw him just this afternoon and he looks like he's lost weight since then. We make eye contact and hold it for a few moments. I have no idea what he's thinking. He pulls out the seat opposite and the bearded ringmaster flips a coin and asks me to call it. *Heads* I tell him. Tails comes up.

Larry takes the Nader and places the nozzle to his temple. Two bullets. There's a good chance Larry might blow his fuckin' brains out here.

I know why he's here, it's nothing to do with reckless bravado. It's another expression I know. Larry accepts there is no such thing as time travel, no such technology exists and won't exist in our lifetimes. In this epoch we have to deal with loss and with our mistakes. We realise that they are set in stone and will shape who we become. For some people this is too harsh a reality to accept. There's no running away from our mistakes here. We're slaves to the smog. Larry is tired of running. He's here for much the same reason as me. We both want to push life against the ropes a little, see how much good luck we got left. Death is the worst possible scenario, but the best outcome might win you some cash to spend on an important addiction that needs tending to.

Larry yanks the trigger and there's a muted click. My turn. I seize the Nader and assume the position.

Maybe there's a different version of me, a version who is picking up a Grammy and playing reunion tours with my old jazz band buddies. Maybe there's a version who got married, had kids, went grocery shopping with his elderly mother. Or maybe there's only THIS version every time? Maybe Ole' Pancake Patterson is unique that way. Maybe I like the thought of being unique. There are a million jazz musicians out there, most of them better than me in my heyday. Better to reject mediocrity and marginalised success, right? Maybe you're different, but there's no way I'd rather go out than listening to the maddening machinery in my ears and contemplating the cool, steel gun against my temple...

ARTHUR FOLGER

The pumpjacks swung to and fro like giant ball-peen hammers driving invisible nails into the earth. It was morning...

... and what a gorgeous morning it was on February Monday 15th man! I remember I had just rolled out of a bar called The Wifebeater, drunken, 100% satisfied in bilious daydreams, you know how it is. I remember feeling young and weightless, like this morning belonged to me and that such an arrogant notion was reasonable and justified as a result of my complete dedication to the premise of L-I-F-E. I was in the mood to foment revolution, completely at one with the great swelling ground-note of the city. Iotas of light came through the high cumulus, jagged, burning, the only light in the universe somehow. I don't know if you've experienced it before, but the air had that certain... aroma too. Woodsmoke, pine needles. The intake of dense, sharp air, the smell of sea at low tide... there's nothing quite like winter's big au revoir, or if there is then *I* haven't experienced it.

I was still brimming with booze but I was goddamn glad to be alive, glad to be out in the quiet streets of my own city. A city that I loved with an immigrant's zeal man.

I remember seeing skinny Mitch at his hot dog cart. We nodded our hellos. I took in the propane heat from his grill as I passed. I heard the sonofabitch laugh fondly at the state of me. I was using the south-facing walls of buildings to keep myself steady. I musta looked hilarious. I could see a fishing sloop out from the coast, it looked so serene. I remember that, although I was still miles from sober, I actually felt okay—in that I didn't have to vomit. My guts felt good, numb... you know? I was even *enjoying* the swirling, romantic thoughts weaving in and out of my half-sunk brain at the time. I thought back to when I first met my wife and how in love we used to be. Then I stopped myself, remembered we were still in love. It was just a different *kind* of love now. But I wouldn't have changed it. *Aaah Deb-o-rah!*–I might've sang. Love was important to me back then, before I realised a man needs to be loved no more than he needs to get, say, a haircut. It just *looks* better when he gets it. And anyway, my cock still yearned upwards at the thought of going home to her and if ever there was a sign that love was present, to me, at least, *that* was it.

I heard the mighty Miles Davis coming from a jazz club that never fuckin slept. I knew it'd be those Ursa Minor cats who had stayed up all night playing recordings with gap-mouthed awe. Ursa Minor man, who'd have thought it? That supergiant and variable star Ursa-fuckin-Minor. Sounds emerge from mounted subwoofers, travelling funnels of noise, seamless expression of the northern sky—the notes spiralling down dwarf ear canals in cyclones of gilded wax. Rotating on imaginary poles! To think, barren, artless Ursa Minor jiving on *Birth of the Cool* man. Music that danced on the trapeze between mind and body, mimicked in a palatal tongue with no vowels. Spit solo…

Music ends

With the orifice mantle and outer teeth we could all hear the people of Ursa Minor lose syntax, fall in love with the *Birth of the Cool*. Those alien bastards made us all realise how good we had it in this place.

I was of the unpopular opinion that the aliens were actually decent enough guys. I'd worked with a few on the freighters. We used to see who could keep their lids stretched apart the longest while knee deep in bilge water. The atmosphere and loss of pressure in the ship meant the cockpit would get insanely dry, dust particles soon started sticking under your tear ducts. Your eyeballs became scratchy, all moisture evaporating from the iridescent orbs. Ursa Minor guys could keep their eyes open for hours at a time. It was amazing.

The palms of my hands came to a wrought iron gate–the backlot of a Chinese restaurant. I was close to home, could see the top of my apartment building. I remember that I wasn't worried about Deborah being pissed off. I'd worked all weekend at the e-resource library cataloguing data and condemning my soul to suicide, she should understand, surely? I worked there so I could pay for our apartment in Newark, so she could have nice things and focus on her weaving. I would tell her that I'd stayed at Larry's place, just a wee pearly white lie. A guy's gotta release the valve once in a while, else he's liable to wake up one morning a homicidal maniac. It kept things well balanced. White lies had their place, I was convinced of it.

Then...

I remember looking up, steadying my neck. A burning ream of light tore across my gaze followed by a bone shuddering KA-BOOOOOM! My ears drums throbbed, my veins felt raked of blood. The smell of winter freshness was gone, replaced by a stink of ozone and salty iron, of smoke and overcooked flesh. The air was bloated with mist. I worked my way through until I was on our street. When the mist eventually cleared I could see the crumbled edifice of my apartment block.

I just knew that Deborah had been inside. I knew she was dead...

Deborah
Yes,
I seek to cut you out from the soil
Wasted flesh, sinew wrapped in silver foil
A statement
The eyes, the mind, the breasts of Lady Lazarus
Yes, yank at the roots, clutch the stem and preen the petals
Put you in a pot and set to boil
Through you,
Ermine eyes,
Jarring the chains, links ring with the sound of
'You do not do, you do not do'
The steam rises in plumes of figure eights
Inhale, clouds like cotton

The words coil ever up and out and *from* the plate
Then,
Blood as oil, yes, and then wait for the oil to appear
Soul as dark as a bathysphere
Or a coal smear
Nigger-eye, the yews fingers,
Exhumed, unpeeled from mother's back
Dark as berries
A statement
The night dance
The dead bell chimes with the name
The return
The memory

Of Deborah…

It was years later man, but I can still remember stealing my way silently through the apartment, peering past each threshold, trying to find the bedroom I'd slept in as a tiny, soft-headed baby. Of course, I'd grown up here but I was surprised by how little I actually recalled of its layout. It was a restless spirit that drove me on.

So I slinked along the corridor plastered with the bad 70's dash-metallic wallpaper—my parents were asleep in their bed, dad snoring like a rusty belt-grinder destroying sheets of aluminium. It would be another 20 or so years until he'd lose his life getting mugged on 8th Avenue at the mercy of a desperate Jam-head sonofabitch. My mother still hadn't succumbed to stress-induced psychosis. This was an idyllic time, even if the aliens had taken over all the industry. I wanted to go up to my parents, touch the dune-contours of their backs beneath the sheets, crawl in between their sleeping bodies and forget about the nightmare that had seized my adult life since inheriting the time machine. Shit…

For a second, I remember savouring the tensed muscles in my stomach relaxing. It was good to see the family unit together again man, and happy, under one roof–then came the iron chill at the base of my fuckin' spine as I remember that it was my job to destroy it all. Kerouac said it best man

'Suppose we suddenly wake up and see that what we thought to be this and that, ain't this and that at all?'

I have never been able to stop thinking about that night. I get plenty of time to think things over these days.

EDUARDO

They say it was a gas leak that demolished both five-storey apartment buildings. The explosion blew out windows over a block away, sprinkled debris onto an elevated commuter railroad track and cast a mushroom cloud of smoke over the skyline. It was insane, took me almost four years to get over Deborah's death—lots of bereavement support group meetings and letting my frustration out on wee promiscuous teenage girls, and in one instance a teenage boy with heavy depression who charmed me with his delicate features! I didn't fuck him you understand, but I let him touch my groin area. I told him I was an alien and that my cock was just an antenna used to communicate with my home-planet. He believed me. Just a white lie, he knew what he was doin'. *Exterminate all rational thought* and all that.

I hit the drink harder and harder, doing Dexedrine just to stay awake, throwing more anthracite onto the fire until I was sliding blindly through life on rivulets of my own bad judgement. When you lose love, at first anyway, it feels like the end of everything. Those four years remain a complete blur. I remember I found some incredible drugs during that period of roaming the wilderness. For a brief time I hung around with a gang of kids who loved Pancake Patterson and were obsessed with synthesising fictitious drugs—Korova milk bars (made with mescaline and opiates) and ephemerol (which were really just mushrooms ground into a paste). We'd take hits from asthma inhalers and store the drugs in ear drop containers. There was even this drug called SOAP that worked just like real soap, but when you bathed with it a microparticulate entered your pores and the high was, well, simply unparalleled–you had to be careful you didn't slump into your bath and drown though.

Those experiences were much less mind expanding than you'd think. People were off fighting in the Kinesis wars battling an alien virus of the mind, but I sometimes think the drugs we took did more harm to a man's brain than the poor soldiers on the battlefield who were getting crushed to smithereens, 10 synapses at a time. Miraculously I somehow managed to keep my position in the e-resource library. The library was the only real job I ever loved, I was grateful to've kept it. I know I bitched about it all the time but compared to other jobs I'd had it was a fuckin' cake walk! Course, before the library I'd worked as a ditch-digger for some Ursa Minor family funeral company, worked as a flunky on a freighter, built with huge girders and an expensive-looking armour plated deflector shield, that hung suspended in space like a hunk of deformed scrap metal—and as a dishwasher on one of those battlecruisers. I never saw any action from the wars, thank god! Every time it was the same deal. After a fortnight on the job I'd get that itch. I'd say–*Arty, why are you condemning your soul to suicide?* Then I'd pack the job in, toss my shovel or my keys or my apron in the direction of the boss and go—*see ya!*–casual as you like. Jesus, I was a ballsy little sonofabitch back then.

At the library I had a real sympathetic boss called Janine who did a great job covering my ass. I told her I was depressed but the truth was that by this stage I was blunt to the core. I will never forget Janine and all the strings she pulled.

Of course I contemplated using the time machine my grandfather gave me to go back in time to save Deborah, to prevent the Kinesis wars from ever happening, but I was terrified to use the damn thing. I didn't really think it worked yano, but I wasn't about to take the chance

Eduardo was a porter working in a basement nearby, an older gent of about 55 with pockmarked skin and big dark eyes. He was originally from LA and claimed to've played Russian roulette with Pancake Patterson. Guess there was no reason to doubt him. I lived with him for a wee while. We originally met through snooker tournaments and started getting together at The Wifebeater every second Sunday when he had the night off.

He was a good man, a decent sonofabitch motivated by a prevailing sense of community. Eduardo had a son called Omar who used to get into a lot of trouble with the gang-bangers in town. Omar was seldom around but when he did show up it was usually to borrow money or to hide a stash of Jam-Caps under Eduardo's mattress. It was a shame.

Eduardo occasionally talked about the Kinesis Battles that swept through the US and detailed the coldness of war seeping into the mud and mortar of trenches in the machine gun night. He saw the brains of his comrades turned to fondue by enemy drones, saw their smoky, scooped-out eye sockets scoured of any recognisable humanity, tasted their burning flesh when the food ran out. Since the wars Eduardo had become a little slow. Apparently one of the viruses had caught him, put his brain in a vice-tight grip until fluid oozed from it like a wrung-out sponge. I don't know how he survived. He couldn't remember either. *What exactly did he fight for? What was he coming back for-a dead wife and a dead-beat son?*

I kept getting up every day for work. Sometimes I'd punch in late but at least I kept showing up. At the weekends I'd play snooker with Eduardo. He kept me on the straight. There's no way I could've pulled myself up from the mire without him. Gradually I got better. Started jogging and taking better care of myself. Deborah became a foggy memory that I was able to bury beneath folds of denial. I started appreciating the smellscapes around me, illuminating gases and banana oil. I still didn't bother with the time machine my cookie old grandfather gave me on his deathbed. I barely knew the guy, for all I knew he was off his rocker on medication. Scientists were doing amazing things, but time travel was never discussed. You never heard it mentioned man.

When Eduardo died of a cardiac arrest I just sort of stuck around at his apartment. I found his body slumped over a chair in an odd position. I remember the sky had gone from grey to hot silver. Quarks of daylight broke through and cast an unflattering luminosity onto the southernmost features of his face. The roads outside were left like shallow rivers once the rain had ceased. I could've sworn I saw my hopes and dreams drift along the gutters. Omar stopped coming round altogether so no one ever questioned my being there. Even the neighbours seemed to think I'd always lived there. In fact, all evidence of Eduardo seemed to disappear from memory when he passed away. The police never checked in, neither did the rest of his family. An ambulance crew came by, took the body and that was that. There was no funeral.

I know, I know—you think I'm a parasite, right? Well, I was lonely and desperate as a fuckin' starving dog. I'd been doing so well to stay sober and motivated. People kept telling me to stay optimistic all the time. Optimistic? Optimistic? *I'm plenty optimistic* I'd tell them! But I remember thinking at the time-*how can anyone be optimistic? I'm a good man. I'm a GOOD man! I'm a good MAN! I told a few white lies in my life and that's all I can be blamed for! Why can't I catch a break, huh? Why do people I know keep dying?* I'd never felt so alone.

THE MURDERER

I explored the darkness farther, turned left down the hallway and saw the bassinet. A doughy faced kid rocked gently in slow-wave-sleep. I *had* to be quick. A violent and prolific murderer was on my tail. The murderer was someone I knew well-as well as the limp 4-month old I'd just scooped up to cradle in my arms.

I made for the open fire escape, tried my best not to alert anyone to my presence. I pulled in the familiar odour of front-load washing machine mould for what I hoped would be the last time. It was a miracle the baby hadn't woken up man, a goddamned miracle–my mother said I'd always been an eerily deep sleeper.

As I was resting my leading foot onto the steel gratings of the outside stairwell, my mother's scream rang out, compressing the air within the inner pillars of my ears until one of the drums P-P-POPPED! I thought about Deborah and the exploded apartment, the only other time I'd heard anything that loud before. In my panic, I accidentally jerked the baby awake and he was now wailing in unison with my mother. *Christ...* All the lights suddenly switched on and I was completely exposed. I stooped under the lower sash of the window and clamped loudly down each level on the platform. The rebound of a gunshot came from up in the apartment. My mother's screaming ceased. I knew the murderer was there and that my parents were both dead-*again*. The howling of stray dogs on the streets kept ice in my blood.

I reached the second floor, slid the final ladder down and descended to the street. The murderer kept eliminating every variation of Deborah, as if he was trying to take away the one thing that gave my life any meaning. Eventually I stopped trying to save her. All I could do man was try to save myself, you know? The baby continued to wail. I heard footsteps from above in close pursuit. I ran. I was used to running away, always escaping...

WALKING THROUGH
THE FIRE

I met Jacob Falcon, a community fireman, antiquarian librarian and small press owner. He thought himself something of a dilettante. I remember he hated all the Ursa Minor chaps, hated the nail bars and hair salons they were opening on every corner at the expense of some vintage bookshop he'd held dear. He smelled of continental cigarettes and claimed to enjoy the taste of madeleines dipped in tea. The press was called 'Black Arrow' or 'Black Adder Books' or something like that. We met during a snooker game in *The Wifebeater*. I seemed to meet all the interesting cats in there. We got to talking (him mainly about his espousal of sweet Buddha) and before long he started pushing me to write a fuckin memoir—*might be therapeutic* he said. *Help you get over Debs* he said. Eventually I sat down with a second-hand tablet in Eduardo's back room and churned out a self-indulgent piece of clap-trap that Jacob reluctantly and begrudgingly sent to press and was later released as a limited edition eBook called *WALKING THROUGH THE FIRE*. The title was a reference to a Charles Bukowski collection and a quote that went—*what matters most is how well you walk through the fire.* At the time I thought it was pertinent as hell. Course, the majority of the book was a pack of lies; in fact the only interesting thing that had ever happened to me was the gory death of my wife Deborah. I'd let it define me. Hideous creatures continued to weave through the geometries of space and into my life.

Point being, I know it wasn't a masterpiece, but Jacob was putting out books by local herbalists and fortune tellers so I hardly think I lowered the quality of his fuckin' stock. He was a little too preoccupied with his upcoming trek out to El Paso to live across the river in a $49 a month cottage with his Buddha Bibles and legume dishes to really have any quality control. *WALKING THROUGH THE FIRE* didn't sell many if you can believe *that*, but it did win me the affection of a young kid called Leo. He was a wannabe writer and I guess he figured that cos I had a book out I was some kind of authority on the subject. '*Follow your inner moonlight, don't hide the madness*'-I told him, but what the fuck did I know? Exactly–nothin'! It was Ginsberg who said that!

Although I detested the book I never went back to erase it from history. Hell, I still wouldn't want it gone, even if I had the fuckin choice, yano?

Leo would always ask me if I had any tips for writing a memoir. I never really knew what to tell the kid but I sure enjoyed the attention and took him under my wing for a time. It felt good to have a protégée, it was different from being in love and being loved... it was more a one-way street that was going in my direction. I didn't have to give Leo a goddamn thing and he still held me in high-regard. I don't think anyone has ever thought that highly of me.

When he was in Eduardo's apartment one night I said to him that going through old keepsakes was a good way to provoke memories, get the creative juices flowing. Leo asked to see *my* memory box. That's when I came across my grandfather's trinket.

-What's that thing?–He asked, his dumb floppy fringe hanging over one side of his face. He must've noticed my reaction, the marble eyes bugging out, nostrils broadening, the complete whitewash of my complexion.

-What is it?–He asked again, a little louder this time with the intention of snapping me out of the trance.

-Something I've been running away from my whole life.

-How come?

-Truth is Leo my boy, if it works I'm not sure I entirely trust myself with its power...

Leo pushed me for more details but I said I was tired and he left.

—— (O) ——

I kept having the same nightmare—the one where I came face to face with myself in a dark alleyway. Whenever I woke it was difficult to disassociate myself from the residue of my dream, the dark shapes streaking the wall with menacing intent. My mother called me. I got up, touched the keypad and the interface screen purled into life. I clipped the electrodes onto both my eyelids. There was a pop of static from the intercom and my mother's voice became clear.

-Your father is dead. Her voice had an inhuman quality that crackled, hissed and fluctuated like what electricity must sound like as it passes through wire.

I hung up.

A few days after discovering the device the e-resource library shut down because of poor business. I was destitute. Suddenly my grandfather's trinket seemed like an escape route...

IDLE HANDS

ALWAYS RUNNING
AWAY-TO-FROM-PAST
I RRUN
SOUR MIND
WOMAN
REACHING +
RUNNING
THE STREETS ARE ALIVE WITH PUNGENT GHOSTS DRAGGED THROUGH NIGHMARES...
LUXURY OF YOUTH...

That night I took the trinket in my hand, fondled it for about half an hour. There was something about it, something dangerous, powerful. It seems ridiculous to say this, but it frightened me in a way I'd never experienced before. It was small and lightweight but had all the patterns of internal cogs and mechanisms visible through its metal frame. It had a tiny monitor that displayed nautical charts and terrestrial range radars, the detail was fuckin crazy. Course, if this really was a time travelling device then in some branching off of this reality all of *this* had already happened and I'd *already* made a decision. Right...?

My grandfather was a senile old coot who smelled of bread chemicals for some reason, a genius probably, but a boor and a heartless sonofabitch at the same time. My dad only ever knew him as this cold, withdrawn cat, always out in his shed trying to build things. I heard he made a robot boy once to replace my dad but it broke down and he never bothered going through all the hassle of rebuilding. For some reason granddad always seemed to like me, even if he didn't show it much, he seemed to have less animosity towards me than the rest of the family. I was secretly quite pleased when he died. I think my dad was too.

Turns out the trinket worked like a drug. There was a tiny nozzle inside about the size of a pinprick and it ejaculated a clear substance in close proximity to human flesh. I fed a polypropylene needle into the nozzle and descended the plunger. The fluid glittered in the syringe barrel like burning intergalactic pulsars. My stomach was in knots but I knew I had to get a hold of myself–*this is your one chance to get out of this place you crazy idiot*–I kept saying. So I mainlined a vein (got that old familiar feeling, ready for a bit of ultraviolence) and administered the time travelling fluid. It's quite a feeling, the evisceration of every particle in your body and its subsequent regeneration in a different region of time.

THE PROPHET OF TOLERANCE

Hell's Kitchen in the 2070s was a profoundly dangerous place, especially at night, man. I knew at this rate I'd surely be spotted. Even at quarter past midnight, The Rite Aid pharmacy lights were still on, the food emporiums and arcades ever-glittering with activity. Extra-terrestrial kids played midnight baseball behind cages (or their own alien equivalent at least) and the streets and alleyways were jam-packed with nefarious Midtown West types trying to secure prostitutes or Jam-Caps. There was nowhere to hide in this part of town when you'd just kidnapped a baby.

I ducked into a narrow alley and tried to catch my breath. I clung to the screaming child with an almost maternal robustness. There was a young kid, maybe seventeen or eighteen years old, sprawled across a bed of garbage, but he was too out-of-it to pose any kind of threat. I rested the baby on my knee and tried to calm it down. A fire engine klaxon annoyed me as it hurtled past.

-Please! I'm begging you, man, just stop crying for a damn minute…

But the restless baby's wails did not falter, man, no siree. The polytonal urban chorus was relentless. The comatose bum jolted back to life, angry that he'd been awoken from his drug-induced slumber. He started gesticulating and babbling drunkenly.

-Hey, you gotta be quiet! Listen, you want some money? You want some, man?

I tried to forward the young bum some crushed notes but the kid was apoplectic. I had to shut him up somehow, considered burying a switchblade into his abdomen, just above his pelvis-after all, who would miss a lousy derelict like *this* guy? Something stopped me, the kid's face was starting to look familiar, even in the eclipsed alley; a certain oblate chubbiness to him that prickled the tiny hairs on the back of my neck.

I remembered, while visiting Elfreth's Alley in 1723, encountering a 17 year old, and impoverished, Ben Franklin newly arrived in Philadelphia from New York. I showed Franklin a hundred dollar bill with his face on it and promised that everything would work out ok for him. The ranting hobo in my wake looked eerily similar, to the point where I actually screwed up my eyes and was about to utter the name–*Ben?*

Suddenly the young bum stopped his inane blethering. A puncture of blood appeared directly between his eyes and trickled down the left hand side of his cheek. The bum's legs buckled and he fell forward, face first, into his bed of trash, his head smacking off of an egg-crate buried beneath. I turned to see a silhouetted figure in the alley.

-Arty… I got you now, you sonofabitch. There's nowhere to go.

AT 64

The murderer stood akimbo, gun nozzle pointed outwards and ready to fire. A series of cables weaved from incisions in his neck and forearms connected the murderer to a control panel on his chest. He plugged the modulator into a port in his temple and started breathing heavily. I looked at the mirror image of my own face and sneered. The murderer's features were slightly greyer, slightly more haggard than my own. We had the same hourglass tattoo on our forearms, although the murderer's was weathered and stretched. He seemed to possess an awful knowledge behind his cosmically weary, cross-eyed stare—visible even through his transparent chronovisor. I didn't bother asking him who he was…

-Why are you doing this?–I begged, glancing quickly at the felled youth sunk half beneath the shadow of the alleyway wall.

-You don't understand…–his voice was bass baritone.

-You're right. I *don't* understand! You've been stalking me through every dimension, murdering innocent strands of Arthur Folger! What's your problem, man?

The murderer sucked in an unfamiliar odour from Hell's Kitchen and gave an exaggerated wince before addressing my question. The whites of his eyes seemed cloudy with the time-travelling substance.

-There's no such thing as an 'innocent Arthur Folger'. In fact, there's no such *person* as Arthur Folger. He has ceased to be a unique, autonomous individual. He's something much worse. He's a card trick, an interdimensional entity who has more in common with a self-replicating virus than a human-fucking-being.

The murderer tensed his finger around the trigger and I knelt, left hand in the air, right still shielding the baby. I realised then and there that there was NO variation of Arthur Folger. It was always just the same thing. It was depressing to see how little I'd changed. I was still running away, still scheming, still looking for the easy route…

-Please man… just… tell me what you've seen. Maybe we can change it?

The murderer broke into a hideous cackle, lifted up his chronovisor. The eyes were actually worse in the harsh radiance of the streetlights.

-It's *way* too late for that Arthur.

-But why?

-You got addicted to the time travelling substance, you're a junky, and like all junkies you can't say no. I have to kill every version, *then* I can finally end it. I can't erase myself without all the rest of you gone too.

-Oh come on, man…

-I've seen the things you've done Arthur, all of them. I'm not talking about that horrendous fucking memoir either. I'm the first, the original, the vessel who carries the burden of all that collected knowledge and experience.

-The original? We've all been imbued with the same shared timeline of memories, you nut-job. We're the same fuckin person!

-Arthur… the future is an ugly reality… and it's all.our. fault.

-Look, you've obviously gone crazy or something… gone insane from years of constantly jumping through the curvatures of space and time. Everyone knows *that* kind of travelling turns your brain into Swiss cheese, man.

I stood back up, took a step forward with my hand out-stretched, trying to make peace yano? The murderer leapt back and waved his gun into the air around my face.

-Don't be a hero! We made too many streams, too many branchings off far too much self-replication has occurred. I can't just kill myself. I'm 64, if I kill myself all that'll happen is that each incarnations of Folger will die at 64, but think how much more damage they could do until then? It's time we started taking some damn responsibility.

I rolled my eyes and exhaled.

-... and we're going to slip up one day soon too, they're going to discover granddad's secret. He didn't even tell our father about it, his own godamned son! That's why we grew up dirt poor but got to live like gods when we grew up... but we're abusing our power as gods. You should've known you couldn't trust yourself, you fuck up. You're a fuck up aren't you? Always have been always will be...

That was true. He went on...

-Take for example, one variation who recently got hit by a taxi cab in 1975. He had no reason to be there, he was just, yano, fucking around in a different decade. The police officer found an iPhone and a Sacagawea dollar coin in his pocket! One Arthur made a flurry of 180 high-risk trades on Wall Street and came out a winner every time! As if *that's* not gonna raise the eyebrows of watchdogs right? Worse than all that, a Victorian opium seller found a copy of this...

The murderer held up a wad of detailed notes...

The murderer and I stared at each other like strangers, neither one able to believe that we'd shared the same experiences, never mind once shared the same ovum. The baby finally stopped wailing and the din from the street became so loud we couldn't ignore it-a slow but consciously motivated clattering of machinery and tortured metal replaced the ruckus and road rage coming from the gridlocked cars-and, instead of human or Ursa Minor voices, ugly and demonic mating calls resonated all along 8th Avenue. Neither of us had the courage to turn and face the new sounds. The murderer's expression was drawn with guilt. He knew he'd changed things again just by killing the young hobo. I wondered if the hundred-dollar bill in my breast pocket would start to vanish. The murderer tried to stay on subject.

-Granddad's precious plans, his legacy, the thing that

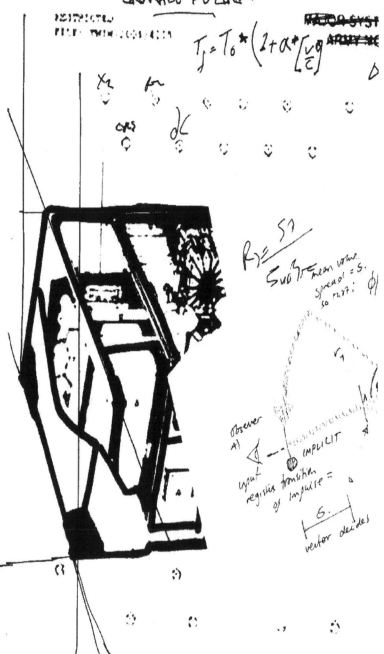

RESTRICTED
FIELD THEMO-COUPLER

$$T_J = T_0 * \left(2 + \alpha * \left[\frac{v}{c} \right] \right.$$

X_2 for

CAS

dC

$$R \geq 5?$$
$$\frac{Sub}{2} = \text{mean value.}$$
spread = S.
so n.xx: ϕ

observer
A)

input
register transition
of impulse = σ

IMPLICIT

S.
vector decides

APARATUS

THIS DESCRIPTION
~~MODEL 61 - G204~~

3D   2D

$$R_s = \frac{S_s}{\sum_{KE} \{ d_{W_j} S d_c}$$

$$t = \frac{0 k_a}{\sqrt{1 - [U^2/c^2]}}$$

?

$$\frac{\partial p}{\partial z} + \frac{\partial}{\partial x} \{ \quad N^2 = 0$$

$$\frac{\partial p v s}{\partial z} + \frac{\partial}{\partial x} (N \sqrt{} \} P_j^{13}_{-q}$$

$$+ \frac{1}{4\pi c} \left[\frac{\partial V}{\partial x^n} \frac{\partial V}{\partial x} \right.$$

$$\frac{[S+\phi]^{exp}}{[S-\phi]^{inj}} = \frac{r_1}{r_2} (F)$$

EXPLICIT

OBSERVER B)

$$\theta_2$$
$$\theta_1$$

$$r_2$$

discussion process of observer B)
ahead

$$\frac{(\mathcal{S}_{ju})}{2 (\mathcal{S}/\mathcal{S}\tilde{w})} = 0$$

$$d_c = \frac{l_c}{V_S} \left\{ 7 - \frac{V_S}{c} \right\}$$

should've won him the goddamned Nobel Prize, just left on the back seat of a chariot after one moron's hilarious fuck-around to Victorian England. I've had to kill innocent men, sonny boy, disrupt the time-line for everyone who knew them! But, hey, don't worry, I'll just keep cleaning up your shit for the rest of frequented time, shall I? When are you guys going to grow up, huh?

-You're speaking as if these were different people or something!

-They are different people, don't you get it? I'm not the same person you are.

He was right about that, too. We'd been eviscerated and regenerated so many times there was no way two variations were ever the same. They simply *couldn't* be.

-I'm older than you guys, remember? You're becoming arrogant, wasteful, skipping through dimensions like reckless assholes. I'm always cleaning up the messes you young guys are making. I'm sick of it, I'm not your fucking dad!

-Hey, no one said you were!

-The only thing left to do is erase Arthur Folger from history. What would granddad say if he saw what we'd done with his creation? What was the *one* thing he told us on his deathbed, huh? What was the *one* thing he stressed above all else?

-Don't tell the government?

-Apart from that...

-Don't use it unless you have to...

-Exactly, but we couldn't help ourselves. We're starting to get sloppy, Arthur, change too much. Fuck, I walked in on twelve Arthur's engaging in a mass orgy with each other last night. What an ego, right? To want to make love to *yourself*! Jeez!

-But...

I had visions of my blood spilling like burgundy wine along the midway.

The worst alternate timeline had to be...

The one with the restaurant owner who fiddled with his apron

Gelatinous structure of alien royalty assuming seat at the head-table.

Owner smiles broadly, nervously at the Royal for what feels like an eternity

Till the muscles on his cheeks begin to quiver.

The busboy brings out the main meal.

Entire spread comprised of kidney dishes

Pitchers and lidded serving bowls

Neatly framed with an array of pewter and old glass tableware.

Restaurant presentation could not be faulted.

The alien Royal is a difficult customer to please when it comes to food.

The busboy's fingertips appear and pinch away the end of the cloche, revealing a marinade-soaked cut of flesh that resembles a thigh.

-This one was an excavator, Arthur Folger. He was quite promiscuous, too, before the mine collapsed on him, good hind shanks.

The owner knows a connoisseur like this is all too aware that the tenderness of the flesh is directly related to the amount of work that a muscle does during the human's lifetime. Without saying anything the Royal stabbed at the plate, impaling a piece of my flesh. The chunk is so large that when he finally does get it down his throat, the alien epiglottis is left raw.

His saliva runs slick with myoglobin which his cranial nerves suck up and ejaculate into
his brain as he savours the strange marriage of gustatory and olfactory stimuli.
A unique palette of flavours apparently. It felt good to be useful.

—— (O) ——

The geriatric variation looked beat, as if all he wanted to do was go home and forget about all this bullshit.

-I just want to die knowing I did the right thing, Arthur. Time travel doesn't grant you eternal life. It prolongs it to an unreasonable degree. Every time an incarnation goes gallivanting through wormholes, I start aging. I think you forget that. I haven't *stopped* aging, Arthur-in fact, I'm aging more rapidly because you guys keep fucking up previous timescapes.

I noticed how fat I'd gotten. *Fat of body, fat of mind*-I thought.

-Ok, look, *Arty*... kill me if you want, but not the baby. You know you can't do it. I mean we're both technically the same person, aren't we? I know *I* can't kill a baby.

-Can't do it? I've tried to kill our mother while she was pregnant about a dozen times just so we'd never be born, but I realised that was too obvious. None of the other assholes obsessed with preserving this sham of an existence would've thought to cover *this* era...

-Well... *I'm* here, aren't I?

-As long as the baby is alive this whole thing will keep going on and on and on and...

I remember my belly flip-flopped. He/I was one mean motherhubbard.

-Please man... I don't want to die.

-I feel sympathy for you. You're young and ignorant. I was the same way, but this is how it has to end, Arthur. Who knows how much damage we've caused to this timeline already? Doesn't bear thinking about... I'm taking responsibility. Maybe, in another place and in another time, you'll realise I'm not the murderer you all think I am.

I noticed his skin was blue, like he'd been kept in cold storage. The murderer wasn't killing me because he wanted to- he really thought he *had* to. He tightened his index over the trigger and the gun went off. A bullet tore through the air in a funnel of energy. Time seemed to decelerate, flow like viscous honey. I tugged away from the slug's trajectory but felt my grasp of the baby slip and I could only watch as it fell gently towards the alleyway-floor. I couldn't move my body quick enough to reach down and re-assume my grasp. Every joint was starched.

For the first time, I looked out at the strange and terrifying world we'd created. I scanned the altitudes; saw eyes staring back at me like darkened windows reflecting the glow of exploded stars and streetlamps. Machines weaved in and out of the crumbling edifice of the old apartment where we used to live with my parents. Time Detectives in trench coats roamed the streets like lonely stereotypes. I dared not look at the shattered image of myself on the alleyway floor.

I observed all this emotionless chaos and smiled. The murderer was smiling, too, feeling, I supposed, completely vindicated. It all suddenly seemed so clear. Both of us revelled in the lights of the oncoming train. Immortality awaits.

I felt my being fade to a spectre, a memory. I saw the dark, disturbed city and, for once in my life, didn't want to be anywhere else. I didn't have to run anymore. I could finally fall into that eerily deep sleep again, the one my mother talked about all those years and minutes and seconds ago...

The only houses left in the city are collapsing concrete tombs. I believe Deborah is in every one of these detonated edifices, like she's been sentenced to a lifetime of eternal damnation. There can be no saving her.

I'd grown accustomed to seeing dead bodies. I saw them all the time on the freighters but my first corpse was when I was a teenager. I remember on my way to the liquor store for my dad, I smelled something rank, something fetid, something fucking badly neglected— round the red brick corner I saw a corpse all slumped in an alleyway.

I moved into the soft shadows. Night always came on quick here submerging everything in the ink blackness of late evening and all the lowlifes were peering out with sickly yellow eyes, just waiting in the wings.

I looked at his face.

A minor politician or a small-time movie star, someone real familiar anyways. Now I think about it, he did look a little like me.

The body was busted up pretty bad but I could still make out the features clear enough.

Who could've done this to another human being-a mob of gangbangers probably, journalists maybe?

I sent my fingers rooting around inside his smooth sockets. I found a gumball and put it in my shirt pocket.

I patrolled the streets every day, I saw a lot-'*can I get a hit?*-the junkies all asked in chorus. I always said no, this was before my own addictions obviously. A blanket of darkness fell over us all, everyone, you too...

- 'can I get a hit?'

The stiff had a nice midnight blue seersucker on, real classy motherhubbard. His wallet was pure cowhide.

Something rumbled in my breast pocket. I retrieved the gumball and held it a few inches from me, watching it vibrate in the palm of my hand. I looked closer. I could make out the intricate details of a city, a whole civilisation trapped inside a murky snow globe-the tiny spires and building tops, the people roaming around the streets like stick insects. After examining the miniature world I popped it back in my pocket. I decided to leave the corpse to fester—nothing I could do for him now.

Back on the streets two kids were playing marbles on the sidewalk I brought out my gumball world and they gathered around me to inspect it closely.

That's when the siren went. The kids scrammed into a grocery store, I had to find cover.

Through the piles of litter and reservoirs of blood pooling at the gutters and spilling down the drains I pushed my legs as fast as they could go.

They were behind me, not far. I could smell them.

I cupped the gumball close to my chest and took a left down a narrow backstreet.

The siren stopped wailing.

I slid through the tight alley and came to a brick wall.

Fuck–I thought as the sound of advancing shoes slowed to a brisk pace.

I turned round and saw a clutch of fuckin' journalists, cameras poised,

This one lousy scumbag wearing a fedora hat with a pen perched behind his ear pushed his way to the front. He held up his notepad of shorthand to the moons light and declared-*'We love your memoir! You can either kill yourself or let us do it? Either way, we're getting our picture.'*

I had no idea who they were or why they had an interest in me. I realise now that I still had a big mouth, even in the future. I brought out the gumball and their yellow eyes lit up like a buckshot rabbit facing headlights.

*–Is that it? Is that the device?–*they salivated.

Then a mangy dog appeared from behind a trashcan and gobbled the tiny city in one gulp.

The journalists watched as the dog wriggled under a plinth and out of sight.

The alley was beginning to stink like a dead man again...

LAST EXIT TO INTERZONE

NOVIKOV

Kip Novikov only ever read two books in high school…

-First you need two magnetic housing units for the dual micro singularities, half-decent cooling and X-ray venting system, um… gravity sensors, four main cesium clocks and probably about three main computer units to properly travel back in time without government issued equipment.

Novikov is talking to no one in particular. He's sitting on a bar stool staring into a reservoir of gin. He's a far-traveled Time Detective but considers himself retired from the business. The bar-keep comes up and rests one of his scaly tentacles on the counter; the other two are busy rubbing the inside of a beer jug with a filthy rag. The bar-keep is a startling sight to behold. While his fourteen eyes flutter in near-perfect unison, the sphincter-like orifice he uses to communicate in his native tongue puckers—a series of rasps and clicks emerge. Novikov seems to understand.

-Yeah yeah, I'm goin…

Novikov heaves himself from the stool and staggers towards the exit. He turns to face the bar-keep

-Hey John, you know what you can do for me?

John, the tentacled, ass-faced bar-keep, straightens his spine in preparation for Novikov's obligatory departing insult.

-You can suck on my plonker!—Novikov grabs a handful of his crotch and shakes it. He turns and fumbles out the door, accidentally tearing off the brassiere of a four breasted female stripper and exposing her large green, milk engorged nipples.

-Sorry love…

Outside, Glasgow is damp. The dome of Kip's bald head

tingles. He should've worn a bloody hat in this weather. The two story high edifices down the left hand side of the street are alive with extraterrestrial festivity. Novikov remembers when he could walk down the street and only see a couple of aliens, most were bums or criminals. Now they're everywhere he looks. The aliens became more successful than the humans (because of their superior intelligence) and soon mankind was relegated to the Cage slums. The irony comes upon him like a cold Martian wind.

Novikov stinks of booze. He ups the collar of his trench coat, hiding the hollow loops beneath his eyes. He now has to make it home to his apartment without catching his own reflection in a store window. A spacecraft hovering overhead makes the large puddles ripple.

An Asian hooker tries looking seductive through sloe-eyes. She gives a come-hither motion with her finger and Kip would be lying if he said he wasn't tempted. Night Slime crouches in the doorways of dilapidated buildings, grunting monosyllabically at passers-by. A bio-luminescent dorsal fin brushes Novikov as he pushes through the alien crowd. It feels good.

It's been almost a year since He's had sex.

He has enjoyed mutually parasitic relationships with numerous men and women (from all different time periods), but things are as grim as they've ever been. He has a girlfriend sure, but she doesn't touch him anymore— Crystal. Her name suggests she's as promiscuous as the city is over populated, but Crystal hasn't so much as looked at Kip's dick lately. Where she had once used her maladaptive oral fixation to please Kip, these days Crystal could be accused of intimate neglect. If Novikov wasn't such an arrogant prick while drunk, his self-esteem would probably be suffering. But as things are, he's content masturbating while she sleeps beside him. Sometimes, when his girlfriend is in a heavy doze, he ejaculates onto her leg. It's a well-known fact that Time Detectives don't have much opportunity for relationships. Kip hasn't traveled anywhere in months, so in the back of his mind he realizes the fault is his. This engulfing inadequacy buzzes around inside his skull in a swarm of negative emotion. He acts out because of it. As dark moods descend upon him, Novikov is constantly reminded of how worthless he has become—to himself and everyone who once cared about him.

Fuck it, he thinks to himself—I'm getting my hole…

-Dalliance-

At the Bordello's pay stand, Kip tries to seem casual. Even a lowlife like Novikov feels like a sinister sleaze-ball when he's paying for sex. Pancake Patterson is playing in the background. He dings the bell but no-one is at the counter. He dings the bell a second him. Nothing. He dings it a third time, pressing a palm extra hard over the mechanism and coughing loudly into his fist.

A vaguely protoplasmic vendor appears.

-Yeah?

-One for the night...

Novikov tosses his passport across the counter. The vendor opens the booklet and glances at Kip's profile.

-A TD eh...?

-Yeah, yeah...

-You want Night Slime?

-Whatever you got I'll take...

The vendor lights up and changes colours from grey to orange.

-I got just the scummy little amoeba whore for you...

The vendor yells into the back in an alien dialect, at which point a cumbersome organism stumbles into the hallway in ill-fitting bra and panties. It slips a silk overall on.

-This is Jody, he's real slutty...-the vendor gives Jody a covetous look.

-Great, great, she'll do great!

-It's a "he" mate...

Novikov doesn't care. He knows that Night Slime are largely sexless creatures created by accident when fragments from Zeta Reticuli met with bacteria in the earth's atmosphere over 20 years ago. There was a time when He wouldn't go near an ET. If he ever had sex, he made damn sure they were human first. Now he could even admit to understanding the perverse pleasures of inter-planetary intercourse.

Kip had just got rid of a particularly nasty alien STD. Night Slime in Glasgow were pretty close to bottom of the barrel, but at least they were clean (for the most part). It's the Night Slime inhabiting the brothels and strip-joints of Dundee you need to watch out for. Most are riddled from birth. Kip found that out the hard way when his dick turned so green it almost had to be amputated. Jody slithers behind the beaded doorway and Kip follows after like a hungry dog chasing promises of treats.

The sky-lit parlour reeks of male intrusion. Novikov's eyes scan the chamber, until they meet the corner of a four poster bed. Jody is resting on the mattress and peeling a long layer of membrane from its chitinous husk. The Night Slime gargles something and Kip thinks the creature is trying to explain itself— he detects an almost apologetic tone from Jody. He sits beside Jody and turns off the light. Even in this socially unconventional situation, he gropes for awkward conversation— once again finding none. Before he knows what's what, the slime covered beast shakes off its headscarf. It slides the long, silk overall from its hunchback and over the top of the dripping red fin on its skull. Kip released his manhood.

The beast impales itself on Kip's cock. He moans, the beast snorts. He's barely touching the sides of the alien sex cavity, but Kip is amazed by how erect he's become. Night Slime were the foulest creatures imaginable, and here he is, stiff as a board for this drooling monstrosity. It *has* been a while! The beast separates its jowls and squashes a hideous face into Novikov's. He feels the fat muscle of its tongue wriggle inside the warm pit of his mouth. He comes and spouts his last thimble-full of fluid onto the Night Slime's right tentacle. He tosses the beast a wad of crushed green notes and pulls up his pants.

It's cold outside. In a climate of such intense global warming, a mild or "cold" day is an occurrence nothing short of phenomenal. The air is difficult to inhale, but Novikov is feeling relieved to've finally bust a nut. He knows it should never have come to paying Night Slime for sex, but a guy's got needs.

Just as things are looking up, he finds himself face to face with someone instantly recognizable, and equally loathsome. Marek Johnston is a fellow Time Detective. He has a pork pie face and skin like corned beef. Sweat frequently sparkles on the surface of his forehead and his hair is disappearing at an uncanny rate.

Kip doesn't share the same attitudes as other TD's— he grew up rough in The Cages. His rise through TD ranks was nothing short of inspirational, achieving a Glasgow Folger University place on the prestigious Dilation Course. Gradually he'd become embittered by the job and the arrogant toffs he had to work with. They always seemed to look down their noses at Kip because of his past, not that he cared.

Johnston lifts a great, fat flipper, inviting Kip to join him in a handshake— Kip refuses.

-Kip, how you been? Haven't seen you in a while?

-Aye, I've been fine…

Johnston looks up at the neon sign beaming with promises of grotesque sexual conquest. Johnston's face softens, he smirks.

-You dog…

-Had to blow off some steam–Novikov tries to remain composed.

-Ha, I'll bet you did! Night Slime though, things must be getting pretty desperate?

-I got a girlfriend…

Johnston squints, all confused. He senses he should drop the subject.

-You know, they're thinking of shutting this place down, income tax violation or something–Johnston reveals piously.

-Tragic…

The notion really does strike Kip as a tragedy, where'll he get sex now?

-Fairfax was asking about you.

-Asking what about me?

-Nothin'… you been quiet these days that's all. You getting work?

-Told you, I'm retired aren't I?

-Right… I forgot. Are you officially retired?

-Unofficially.

-Right, I forgot.

No one really retires from this business. Most continue to journey the tears of space and time until they drop dead from motion sickness.

-Well, don't forget again.

Kip senses his own abruptness and suddenly feels like he has to get out of the conversation quick.

-Look I gotta go. See you…

-The Cages-

The Cages are the worst part of Glasgow. Kip grew up here and that accounts for his sense of working class resentment towards the establishment. The Cages were put up in place of the old Red Road flats, replacing one bedroom apartments with steel mesh cubicles. A tower of them makes up the project and Novikov can well remember his rough upbringing trapped inside. Each resident pays ten Euro-Rubles for a Cage, 30 for a family of three. Novikov shared a Cage with his sister Alex. Masturbating was impossible inside the Cage because each frame was joined at the grill— Kip neighboured his father's Cage.

A group of hoodies are playing beside a pile of burning tyres. Novikov doesn't feel threatened, until he realizes one of the youths has an actual photonic crystal gun in his hand—a conspicuous weapon with government cast-iron butt and a Punch-Hole CTI Digit Handler. The Krasnikov tubes divide into separate time-lines; these are so lethal because vacuum fluctuation will destroy the second tunnel after only a few minutes. Inexperienced time travelers are disintegrated and erased from the memories of anyone who's ever known them. Kip approaches the young man with the gun and, rather fearlessly, snatches it from him. One of the boys with a face of malnourishment jumps from his swing to confront Novikov.

-What you doin mister? Giez that back ya prick!

-Where'd you get this?

-What's it to ye, cunt?

Kip feels a sudden need to explain himself to these children.

-You think I don't know this place?

-You're a fuckin TD, you're probably fae Bearsden or something!

-I'm *from* here! I used to play by the old swing enclosure over there...

-Yer baws!

-I mean it!

Kip pockets the crystal gun and tells the kids to keep their noses clean, to which he receives a foul mouthed reply for his troubles. Kip's Alert Watch buzzes and a robotic voice squeals something about "ALERT, NEXT ASSIGNMENT!"

Novikov groans and checks the details.

-TANGIERS, MORROCO, 1954...

Novikov, in his tenure as a TD, has made a few celebrity friends. He knows instantly who's beckoning him from this particular region. It could be only one man— Bill Burroughs. He and Burroughs became acquainted during a drug raid of Jack Kerouac's Manhattan apartment, where the cops seized around one hundred dollars-worth of heroin and Benzedrine inhalers. Novikov saved the day by blasting a vortex in the wall with his photonic crystal gun. Everyone found the whole experience really trippy and told Kip to drop by anytime, he was always welcome. Kip sends Crystal a Z-SMS reading simply– *"I'm away working. Back home late. You'll know It's me coming in when you feel that unexplainable lurching in your belly and your lady-bits begin bleeding stigmata uncontrollably. X"*

He flips the eyeshade of his chronovisor down and puffs out a gust of exasperation.

Kip steps from the hyperboloid and his feet touch sand-this is Tangiers alright. There are as many middle aged Caucasians as there are Keffiyeh sporting, thawbed arabs. He heads towards a little bistro with a load of people sitting outside on the terrace, all smoking from pipes and, probably, engaging each other in profound intellectual discussion. One fellow, a bald chap with bifocals and a fedora hat on, shelters himself under a parasol from the desert heat. He strikes Novikov as familiar. It's Bill. His eyes seem weak with grief and guilt, but he expresses faint joy at the sight of Kip.

-You came!

Burroughs gets up from his chair and embraces Kip.

-Let me just, touch your face… I wanna make sure I ain't just tripping… you're really here?

-It's me Bill, you look like you've been tarred and feathered…

-I didn't know where else to turn…

-Relax…

-Let's not talk here. Let's go back to my place.

In Burroughs coastal villa, Kip and Bill sip cognac and puff from a carb pipe. On the sand-blasted landscape outside, young Africans are dredging for anything valuable.

-A real panacea for pain eh?–says the Time Detective redundantly. Burroughs nods absent-mindedly. Novikov blows a prodigious smoke ring into the air and asks his friend what ails him.

-I got a problem Kip... I fucked up...

-How?

-In Greenwich Village, Kammerer–you remember him right? He was there that time the Feds busted in on our drug party?

-Sure, nice guy...

-Yeah well... since the last time I saw you, I killed two people... one being Kammerer...

-What?

-I killed him...

-Why??

-I was high... he wouldn't shut up... he just got to me, I hate fuckin loud mouths. Kept making advances on Lucien... if I didn't pop the little cunt, even Carr admits he would've done it eventually.

-Who else have you killed?

-You remember Joan?

-Shit... I knew that.... .

-Anyway, my pal Lucian Carr is taking the rap for me. He's a sweet soul to do time like that, but the agents are already after me... they're here Kip...

-Where?

-In Tangiers! They know, I'm tellin' you!

-Listen Bill... I can't physically take someone else back in time with me...

-Can't you go back and warn me?

-Warn you not to kill two people? I dunno Bill you were always kind of a stubborn arsehole...

-Come on!

-I can't Bill. Even I wouldn't dare fuck with the fabric of pre-set time! It could cause an Event Horizon! Fuck that for a game oh soldiers!

-If you can't go back, you can go forward right? You remember that book you said I was gonna write, the masterpiece? I need you to take me to the point in time where I actually write it. Agents aren't gonna suspect a respected novelist.

-You won't exactly be respected right away...

-Huh?

-Never mind. It's another year till you start to properly write it Bill, relax! I've seen the future, you're a legend, immortal, fuckin untouchable.

Burroughs breaks down.

-Now what's wrong?

-God... I... I wasn't being completely honest...

-Jesus Bill, about what?

-About only killing two people...

-What'd you mean?

-It's the ugly spirit Kip...

-Talk sense man!

-Jesus, they cut off your hands in this country if they find out you killed someone...

A fresh faced Moroccan catamite appears in the doorway draped in djellaba

-Shall I bring him in Master Burroughs?-Says the boy reticently.

-Yes Kiki... bring her in...

The boy disappears into the room across the hallway. A moment passes and he comes back through dragging a long object wrapped up in blood soaked linen. He drags it to the centre of the room and lets the bottom half thud to the ground in a crumpled mess–it's obviously a body.

Kip inches towards the sheeted corpse and kneels down. He gently unwraps the skull area and almost chokes on his own surprise. Kip stands up and backs into the corner of the room, realizing he is a little terrified of Bill Burroughs now.

–Who is that?

–A girl, Joselito, who snuck into my home. I thought she was an agent…

–You've totally fucked up your timeline Bill…

–You saying I might not write that novel now???

–I'm sayin you WON'T write it…

–But…

–When you killed Joan Vollmer in 51, the experience was so shocking, so uncharacteristic that it set in motion a state of mind which you claimed helped you to write Naked Lunch… but now you're just a fuckin' serial killer… that's your destiny, stipulated, unchangeable.

He lowers the chronovisor and scans the future threads William Burroughs has created.

–Yup, it's completely altered…

–What are?

–Your future timescape…

–Why has it changed? You can't know that! Amphetamine Psychosis, that's what this is. I'll book myself into Bellevue when I get back to New York…

–I've seen this thread of time, you end up as hated as Bundy… and you don't stop killing either.

–I kill *more* people?

–Lots more…

Burroughs slumps to the floor. Kiki comes over and places a consolatory hand on his master's shoulder.

–What the fuck am I gonna do?

The large lenses of his spectacles have become fogged; he removes a handkerchief from his breast pocket and rubs away the mist. Kiki gives him a steaming bottle of something which Burroughs proceeds to glug down.

-What's that?

-It's Yage, tetrahydroharmine. I can tell what you're thinking now.

-What?

-It gives you clairvoyance... and I'd thank you not to consider stealing my ottoman.

-I never said I wanted to steal your ottoman!

-Not out loud you didn't, but I heard!

Burroughs begins slurring his words with a face succumbing to chronic botulism.

-I went to Harvard you know, I think I know what's good for me ya bum! You scoff at telepathy. Even for a cunt from the future you're arrogant?

-Ok...

-By the great ghost of Bhoot, my psionic impulses are tingling. You want me to get all clairvoyant on your ass, huh? My strength is bouncing off a torsion field.

-Ok, you know what I want Bill?

-An enormous sandwich of pure human meat?

-No... I want to help you out Bill!

-Really?

-There's something I can do.

-What? You mean it?

-There are two of you Bill... one who kills and one who loves...

This statement strikes Burroughs as poetic, profound: he hasn't seen *Apocalypse Now*, it isn't made for 10 more years!

-You're a pal Bill, you get me good gear. Here in the future they don't make Benzedrine. You keep supplying me on tap with the drugs I want and I'll fix this for you...

-What you gonna do?

-I'm gonna make you a novelist.

TWO

-Last Exit...

In 1958, Hubert Selby Jr begins writing his magnum opus, *Last Exit to Brooklyn*. Kip has decided that a permanent supply of Beat-era drugs is enough to challenge his occupational integrity. He plans to steal Selby's manuscript and return to Tangiers where Burroughs will pass the novel off as his own.

Selby has some of the strongest future threads, some of the most flexible too. He can deviate from one path and still be on course for becoming successful and published.

On the 69th street pier in Bay Ridge, Selby is engaging in a vicious bare knuckle brawl with a fisherman. Novikov took a generous hit of junk before leaving Morocco. Burroughs gave him a hybrid concoction of Yage and uncut morphine for the journey, bad idea! When the swirling portal closes behind him, Novikov loses footing and goes crashing into the Narrows strait. Kip's inertial frame of reference is jolted and he feels his guts heave outward as water floods inward through his nostrils. For a moment, he allows himself to anchor. He suspends in the freezing harbour, indecisive about whether he should swim to safety or simply sink to the harbour floor. Crystal pops into his head, perhaps he misses her? She doesn't put out so that couldn't be it. His head descends to reruns of his tryst with the Night Slime

–Jody, was it... ?

The ice cold temperature brings a return to sobriety and clarity. Novikov drags himself from the water and sees Selby jostling around on the quayside. The fisherman he's battling is a tough and weathered sea captain–compared to the frail, 5ft-nothing Selby, the fight seems a total mismatch. The captain twists his hairy fists. Selby lunges at the captain's gut, hammering two hard punches which crack loudly. The captain goes down and Selby spits a gob of saliva at his crumpled body. Everyone cheers but Selby just grabs the captain's wallet, takes out a ten and walks away.

Kip, more than impressed by Selby's moves, tries to approach him. He is suddenly aware of a celebrity-awe creeping upon him as he makes eye contact. *Last Exit to Brooklyn* was an epoch-making event in his life, suggested to him by Mrs McLaughlin in English class. Selby seemed to know what life was like in the Cages, how tough life was. He became instantly obsessed.

-That was some fight...
-Who the fuck are you?
-Kip...
-I'm Cubby, do I know you?
-No sir, but I'm a big fan.
-A big fan of what, my fighting?
-... sure...
-I'm on Nandro... it keeps up my strength. I'm also usin' a lot of heroin so my hands are numb as heck. I can get a couple of good jabs to the rib cage before it wears off, by then I've already softened them up and the hard work is done.

Selby is totally out of breath.

-I ain't got enough lung capacity apparently... so say the fuckin murderers at Marine Hospital anyways...

Selby is an odd character. His impish stature and tough talk make for a hilarious, highly oxymoronic image. That this man is possessed by literary genius seems inconceivable—Selby is like the local nutter with PTSD, mocked by awful memories of childhood and war. Novikov is intrigued by the notion of Selby and Burroughs coming together in a fist fight.

-So what can I do for you?
-Oh um...-it occurs to Novikov that in the process of his plan, he has forgotten to perpetuate a suitable backstory for himself.
-I'm a... tourist...

-No shit, with that accent, you fuckin Irish or something?

-Not quite. Scots-Russian…

-Fuck, I guess you'll be lookin for the nearest bar then, huh?

Kip agrees, seeing this as a perfect opportunity to get close to Selby and create an illusion of trust.

At a rough bar called The Tarantula's Nest Kip and Cubby drink stale, frothless beer from Styrofoam cups. Cubby looks ill. He's gaunt and pale and doesn't look like he's enjoying his alcohol. His skin is a transparent film over the skeleton beneath, he looks vulnerable, as if a simple flu virus could disable his immune system and kill him instantly.

    -You ok-asks Kip.

    -Sure, sure...

    The two men sit in silence until Selby speaks again

    -You wanna try something that'll really knock your socks off?

    -Sure-Kip is sincerely interested.

    -Ok, well meet me tonight and we'll seal this deal together.

    -I don't really know Brooklyn...

    -Christ pal, only the dead *really* know Brooklyn.

    Kip doesn't *get* the statement and his apparent confusion riles Selby.

    -Fuck man, if you need a place I guess you can crash with me. But I'm warnin' ya, it's a one-bedroom apartment and I got no electricity. I got a bitch for a wife and a screaming kid that don't take breast milk.

    -Thanks...

    -Don't get me wrong... I love my wife...

    Kip smiles gratefully and swallows down a lake of bitter, piss-tasting beer. After this big drink, he feels like he needs to spit. When he lifts his head back up, Selby is glaring at him distrustfully.

    -So what's your story? I mean really?

-I told you, I'm a tourist.

-I don't buy it. Tourists don't end up in the part of the city you wound up in, unless you're a Scandinavian or a Greek...

-They do if they don't know where they're going.

-You got a kind of weird confidence to you. If I wasn't so intrigued by it, I'd knock your teeth down your throat. You get the Poles of Greenpoint, now you guys are here to cram up more condominiums?

-No...

-Yellow Hook is a shit hole, when you guys gonna learn that? I oughta punch you in the throat for your fuckin dumb stupidity!

The threat barely registers from this strange little man. Admittedly, Selby was tough, he had the moves to go with his mouth, but the stark image of him sitting across the table, frail and world weary, failed to stir any fear. Kip knew that Selby underestimated him (maybe). He too was a tough character. He'd seen and done things even Cubby couldn't dream of.

Unlike Glasgow, the New York sun is hot and hostile. Surrounded by the denizens of the housing projects–kids are playing hopscotch and "red light, green light" on the sidewalks, hoodlums called Vinnie deal drugs in the shadows, gangs fire linoleum projectiles from carpet guns behind the safety of their parents' apartments... Glasgow and New York share a criminal charm. A transvestite hooker waves at Selby from across the street.

-Who's that?

-That's Georgie. Saw the poor broad gang raped just last month, saved her ass.

-Jesus...

-Yeah, trannies are the last bastion of ridicule. The only minority the blacks, whites, straights and fags can come together and shun.

Novikov looks at Georgie, he feels a spark of electricity dance along each of his vertebrae. Selby spits onto the side-walk and gives a guttural cough.

-Come on, let's get a bagel.

Cubby fishes around his pocket and brings out a mess of keys. He locates one and sticks the door with it.

-I never been to Scotland before.

-You're not missing out on much, it's a fuckin shite hole.

-Fuck, can't be any worse than this crap-chute.

-You'd be surprised.

A voice, stage left, cries out Cubby's name. Another junk-hungry guy called Lonny. Behind a smoldering cigarette, he has a smug face, like he's consecrating the Eucharist.

-There is no hope man... only Gods will...-Lonny says impenetrably. He leans on the brick wall by a liquor store. Selby is glad to see him.

-Lonny, you old fuck!

-Come on Cubby, language man, language. You got no class or what?

-Yeah, yeah. You got the shit?

-You bet your ass I do. You got money?

Selby pulls out a zip-loc bag of notes and retrieves two 5 dollar bills.

-You're going to heaven Hubert Selby Jr.

-I don't think so Lonny.

Cubby comes back with his baggie of drugs, glowing in a new optimism.

-Good old god boy!

-He doesn't strike me as the religious type-Kip confesses.

-Oh yeah, he's a total bible thumper, has been all his life. When we were at school, I went to the navy and Lonny was torn between becoming a preacher or a drug dealer.

-Huh...
-You'll never find an atheist in a fuckin foxhole pal...

Selby starts boiling the contents of the baggie. He sucks through a tube and passes it along to Kip–who takes a big hit. The taste is strange, like bad faucet water. Selby's drugs don't have that refined edge to them, not like the stuff Burroughs gets his hands on — where you can see and touch the planets set like jewels in space. Philip K Dick always had some good drugs, but Kip didn't visit him much anymore. Phil was fun for the first hour, and then steadily became a little paranoid and weird. Instead of swirling in a junk euphoria, Kip allows the drug to filter through his system like a retrovirus, slipping him into an anxious, sleepy depression. Selby's drug sits thick in the bloodstream, decaying the marrow beneath and destroying the brain cells above.

-Woah... bad junk...-Kip says sluggishly.

Selby's eyes reel to the back of his head, it's the happiest Novikov has seen him all day. He could pass out himself. He does pass out. A night without stars...

Novikov wakes up and sees Selby removing his slacks. Kip, wet with perspiration and chronically disorientated, feels like he's been cut out of a dead horse–.

-I'm headin off to bed.

-Bed? It's only 7 o'clock.

-I got work tomorrow.

-Work?

-Yeah, at the gas station. How'd you think I support my family dumb-ass?

Selby disappears into his bedroom. A cot with a murmuring baby rocks gently by the open apartment window. Novikov wonders where Selby's wife is at? The apartment itself is a little rundown—scrunched up paper balls litter the carpet. The heat outside is almost intolerable, even this late in the evening. A turtle could be boiled in its shell if left outside too long. In a rare moment of compassion, Kip notices the baby squirming under direct sunlight. He pulls himself to his feet, shifts the cot and draws the curtain. Then he bends over to retrieve one of the paper balls; it's a title page reading in thick, hard type—

-The ~~Queer~~ Queen is Dead...

-JACKPOT!

-What you doin?

Novikov swings round, still a little listless, and the letter sheet floats to the carpet, at one again amidst the sea of paper below.

-Oh um... I...-Kip hadn't expected to see Selby standing in the doorframe. Fortunately he doesn't seem angry.

-That's just the title page, I got a whole manuscript I been workin on. You read much?

Kip thinks for a moment.

-I read select works...

-I'm just dying to get it published. I dream of my stories ending up in Provincetown Review, you must think that's pretty dumb?

Kip feels guilty. How can he snatch this man's (one of his idols!) future away, just like that.? Because he's Kip Novikov, cunt, that's why.

-Those motherfuckers at the New York Times won't publish me, but one day they'll print my obituary, you mark my words!

-Normally I wouldn't doubt you Cubby...

Selby sighs theatrically and scratches his crotch.

-Yeah, well anyhoo, I'm off for some shut-eye. Have a good one, n' don't steal anything...

When Selby is gone, Kip begins frantically searching for the manuscript. He turns over drawers and cupboard contents, but there's no sign of *Last Exit* Kip peers into Cubby's room. He's snoring aggressively already and there is a mound lying next to him which Novikov assumes to be his wife. In the process of scanning the room he notices something — the jagged edge of a paper stack by his bedside. Kip sneaks in, artfully dodging the array of crap strewn across the bedroom floor. Standing over Cubby now, he lifts the thick manuscript, the front cover says– *Last Exit to Brooklyn* He looks down at Selby, who is so deep in heroin slumber. He seems so frail in bed-this book really would give him a whole new sense of purpose. But then Kip remembers Burroughs promise, those drugs really are something else after all! Kip thinks about the bad junk Selby gave him and suddenly the whole operation seems perfectly justified. He sneaks out of Selby's bedroom with the manuscript underarm.

-Hey... what you doin?

Novikov swerves round, piston-like. Selby is up, erect on the mattress like a reanimated corpse springing back from the dead. Kip panics and fumbles for his photonic crystal gun. Selby is out of bed and advancing with a crazed, confused look in his eye. Eventually Kip gets the gun ready and blasts a hole in the apartment wall. Selby has frozen in the doorframe, mesmerized by the churning, multi-coloured gateway to other regions of time. Kip shoots an apologetic glance in Cubby's direction before throwing himself head-first into the vortex.

He's done it...

-The 3 Stigmata of Bill Burroughs-

Back in Tangiers, Burroughs is lurking in a marketplace alley. Kip emerges from the vortex with a victorious grin on his face. He holds Selby's manuscript aloft like a world cup winner presenting the trophy to home support. Burroughs motions out of the shadows, he perks up.

-Is that... ?

-Yup.

Burroughs is giddy, he looks on the verge of joyous tears.

-What's this about anyway?

-I told you, it's a filthy, controversial, inspiring nightmare. Take a look.

Burroughs takes the novel, flicks through each page ruthlessly. He pulls a face like he's eaten a bad clam and hands Selby's masterpiece back in disgust.

-What. The. Fuck?

Confused, Novikov sits on a step outside a market stall.

-You, um... you don't like it?

-It's a piece of shit! I fuckin hate Brooklyners

-I don't think you appreciate...

-He doesn't punctuate!

-Ok, but...

Burroughs snaps and throws his hands in the air.

-Ahhh, shut up! This was all a con right? Setting me up, trying to ruin my reputation? You're an agent, right?

-I'm not Bill, I swear!

-You're no Time Detective! You're a fuckin loon!

Novikov stands up from the step, making no effort to conceal his offence.

-Excuse me?

Burroughs mood changes. Now he's frightened, intimidated, and apologetic.

-Ok, now easy there... I wasn't trying to get a rise out you...

-This is insane.

-Now wait, I can offer a prognosis if you want?

Kip folds his arms, becoming increasingly impatient. Burroughs has obviously had a hit of something very recently — Kip wants some too.

-The psyche creates your sense of beliefs to protect you from the part of reality too awful for your mind to perceive, right? Reality is also very subjective.

-These broad, sweeping statements aside, you've failed to inspire me with your words Bill.

-What if I were to call you mentally divergent?

-I'd say you'd confused my ability to manipulate time and space for a nutter, which I am not.

Burroughs shuffles closer.

-You're using parts of your psyche to escape certain realities in your life, constructing new truths, albeit convincing ones, in an effort to survive. It's all survival.

-No Bill. You've seen me create worm-holes. You know I wouldn't lie. You're not crazy are you?-Kip wonders how crazy Burroughs *really* is.

-Now, I'm sorry Bill, but I'm more than a wee bit insulted by this petulance. Do you know the effort it took to get you this? Aren't you grateful that I did you this favour? That I used my unique means to its fullest effect, endangered my life? Ruined a man's empire for you? Does that mean fuck all to you Bill?

But Burroughs isn't listening. He's busy batting at a mosquito.

-Bill!

He quickly snaps to attention.

-Sorry. I got no energy Kip, I'm limp on skag... these peddlers came round and gave me Majoun... then Eukadol, it's phenomenal but I'm utterly junked-out...-Bill sits down.

-Jesus Bill...

-You should know by now I thrive on all manner of degradation, it's my life-blood, it's my protein...

It occurs to Kip that he needs a shower–bad. Even through his gabardine trench-coat a continent of sweat has reached the outer surfaces. Burroughs is shifting on his seat, trying to suffocate an itch.

-Hey, I thought a cool title might be *Confessions of an American Opium Eater*

-I told you, Ginsberg gives you the title!

-Why don't *you* just tell me what it is yourself?

-Cos it'll disrupt the fabric of your timeline AND mine!

Burroughs accepts defeat.

-Ok, you win. I'll use this piece-of-shit manuscript too. I guess I trust your judgement.

Kip observes Bill. He can practically hear the malignant insanity eating away inside Burroughs' head. It would be a bad idea to irk Bill anymore.

-I best be off then.

-Not before I give you your payment.

They head back to Bill's place to pick up Novikov's payment. Burroughs disappears into a water closet and returns with a canvas sack full of something.

-What's that?

-Pickled lemons. They're popular over here.

-I don't get it...

-It's your reward, I said I'd pay you and by George I'm a man of my word!

-You said you'd pay me drugs...

-I did?

-YES!

-Shit. Well, I just don't know what to tell you. I ain't got none left.

-Fuck off!

-I mean it, I'm cleaned out.

-Where did your supply go?

Burroughs looks shamefully at his feet.

-I took 'em all.

-I'm leaving Bill. Don't expect to see me for a long time. Despite Burroughs half-hearted appeals, Novikov has already blasted a portal in the wall. Kiki comes in topless, a strange fear in his eyes, like a trapped animal terrified of its owner. Kip has been friends with Burroughs for the longest time. He's made his own time-line fraught with uncertainties from all the to-ing and fro-ing. It all seemed worth the hassle before, now he realizes he's been a fool this whole time. How could he have had such a poor judge of character? He concludes that (excluding his own insatiable desire to consume pure psychedelic opiates) in a way he has been tricked. Burroughs isn't the man he once was. In fact, he doesn't even seem human. Harlan Ellison would kick this guy's ass, Cubby would kick this guy's ass! Kip feels like part of Selby has somehow followed him through each vortex. Amidst a torrent of guilt, Kip motions towards his gateway. He dips one foot into the swirling vortex, sighs, and then plunges himself completely...

Kip wants a drink. If he can't rely on his friends to come through for him, he'll acquire his own means of escape. He's still sore about Burroughs but reckons a night on the raz will banish his bitterness. Truth be told, he really does feel worse about stealing Selby's manuscript than he thought himself capable of. In a strange way he sees Cubby as a kindred spirit. How would He feel if some time traveling cunt blithely deceived him then stole his future? Kip can't shake the feeling of being followed, that some element of his psyche has been left behind in Selby's time... or Selby's presence has traveled through to the future. It hangs over him like shadows cast from a Qliphoth tree.

He stops in at Shannon's Bar. A TD (Andrei Arsenevich) is receiving oral sex in the side alley, from a repulsive creature with heavy insectoid features. Kip can't help but stare as the creature snares the TD in a web of alien silk and publicly mugs him. He doesn't give a toss; the TD probably had it coming.

John the bartender is pulling pints and cleaning beer mugs, fully exploiting the multi-phalanges at his disposal. John catches sight of him and groans loudly. Kip pulls out a barstool, sits down and orders a gin and tonic with coke. Even here in this futuristic, multi-species waterfront dive, Kip sees Selby in the darkness, behind a fog of cigarette mist. John sticks his ugly ass face into Kip's.

-What've I told you pal?

-Just get me a drink eh? Do your job and quite the belly-aching.

-Novikov, you're a fuckin wreck in here every night. You scare away my customers, you don't pay for booze and you're always having a pop at the ET's. Frankly I've had enough of you!

Kip slams two fivers onto the counter and leans over to suck beer straight from the tap. John allows him to do this, snatching up the money and stuffing it into the till.

-Alright, you can stay... but be sensible about it tonight.

Kip releases the beer tap and comes back up for air, his chin a beard of foam.

-Alien beer is the best, there, that's not racist is it?

John keeps on cleaning glasses. The music in Shannon's is alien too; all clicks and white noise frequency. Kip tuts audibly, even a little tipsily at this early stage.

-It's a good thing the alcohol is good, cos ET music is fuckin shite!

Kip feels a sudden itch beneath his belt. When he scratches, the itch turns to a sharp pain. Clutching at his groin, Kip darts to the Male Humanoid Defecation Facility. He locks himself inside a cubicle and frantically drops his pants, his underwear follows. He can't believe his eyes. Looking down, he sees that his penis is almost entirely green, the shaft has wilted into a sea shell and his testicles have retreated inside him

-What the FUCK?

The closer he inspects it, the more grotesque the state of his penis seems. Small growths are mushrooming along the underside of the glans. Now that He is aware of them, they become insufferably itchy. The off-yellow/green complexion of his member is akin to the glowing contents of a radioactive drum.

-Fuckin Night Slime!

-Just need you to fill up these containers with your 1s and 2s.

Doctor McLeod holds out two glass beakers. Kip, red faced, accepts them. Fortunately, McLeod and he go way back, they were both in the squadrons together during the last Serbian conflict. Kip showed up at the army quarantine base with a laser-shot wound to the shoulder.

They shared an interest in alcohol and lower league amateur football.

-Any jobs recently?–asks Doc McLeod ticking boxes on a chart of another patients systolic readings. Kip has disappeared behind a drawn curtain and is filling up the first container with a measure of his urine —the passing of which stings like hell, but he keeps a good lid on it.

-Aye, made the big mistake of helping out that scoundrel William Burroughs.

-Not again.

-Ach, he got himself in a total mess, made an arse of his time-line. I fixed it though.

-Good stuff. How is the auld cunt anyway?

-He's not as charming as I remember… he's more like a murderous despot with his finger stuck on a shot gun trigger.

Kip reappears with a brimming beaker.

-D'you want the shite sample just now?

-If you wouldn't mind? I'll get this prepped for testing while you brew up a bum buster.

Novikov slithers into the toilet and does the deed.

The doctor slaps on a pair of rubber gloves and takes a handful of yellow powder.

-What's that?–Novikov asks with sincere curiosity.

-It's the basic compounds found in your urine big man.

-Modern medicine eh?

McLeod grins and takes a glug of Irish coffee.

-I'll test it on my Acid/Alkali Machine.

The doctor pushes a button and a curtain lifts to reveal a subdued monkey in a cage. He tosses the powder in the monkeys face and it yowls.

-It's acid alright–the doc clarifies. Even Kip is horrified by this mistreatment. The doc acknowledges his disgust.

-It's a little jolting at first, I admit. Believe me, every time I ruin a monkeys face it takes away a little part of me.

Keen to get out, Kip hands the doctor his next sample.

-Hmm… this looks industrial.

He tosses the sample in the monkey's eyes again.

-Stop doin' that!–Kip protests.

-That's a bad STD you've got mate. You've not been bonking Night Slime again have you?

-What if I have?

-Ok, I'm not here to judge. The Blinded Monkey Scale suggests that's erosive Herpes. Here's a salve for it. Use it twice a day for three months and for god sake don't shag any more bloody aliens!

-I'll try.

-Don't try, do or do not…

-Think I've been invaded enough for one day.

-You're lucky I didn't ask for a spunk sample!

—— (O) ——

Back home Crystal is waiting for him in bed.

-I've missed you–the naked girl says, covering herself up with the duvet. She looks supernaturally attractive.

-Aye right.

Any affection directed at Kip these days is automatically deemed spurious. However, he has already forgotten about his erosive herpes.

-I mean it, come sit with me.

Her certitude is encouraging. Kip approaches the bed somewhat distrustfully. She lets the duvet drop, kicking the sheet to her ankles in one single all-revealing motion. Crystal's breasts are perfect, global and pink. Kip had forgotten how attractive she could be. Crystal swings round so her face is inches from his. Her breath is hot with the residue of aphrodisiac food.

-You seem a little tense…-she says.

-I'm just a bit stressed, what with the proliferation of nuclear weapons, global warming, etcetera…

Kip feels his erection fatten and stiffen up and before any hesitation is allowed to breed, he has already begun…

—— (O) ——

Lying in bed, Kip can feel sleep set upon him, for the first time in a long time. Intimate sex can be a wonderful tonic for insomnia. Just as he's slipping deeper into a warm slumber, he hears a clattering come from the bathroom. Crystal, apparently unperturbed by the noise, snores away noisily like a deranged pig getting its throat cut open. Kip slides out of bed and heads towards the bathroom. He figures it'll be something trivial, bathroom utensils falling from a cabinet, a cat toppling everything in its wake…

He gets to the doorframe and looks in. Behind the shower curtain, something is wriggling around in the tub. He approaches cautiously and begins peeling back the curtain. Burroughs is lying in his bathtub, naked like a hideously deformed new-born covered in amniotic fluid. Resting on the toilet seat is a photonic crystal gun. Kip recognizes it but knows it's not his own (he calls his own gun Cassandra). He remembers the weapon he took off those Cage kids and realizes he must've left it in the past — a potentially cataclysmic mistake.

This world is not meant for past specimens like Burroughs, their bodies cannot adapt to the intense tropical climate or process the hoard of alien communities dotted throughout the country. Kip goes up to Burroughs, who is still shivering like a starved greyhound.

-What the Jesus-fuck are you doing here?

Burroughs looks up and grins.

-You gotta help me Kip…

Novikov groans and snatches a towel from the wrack.

-Awe no! I helped you enough man, no way…

-Please Kip... it's Kiki...

-What about him?–Kip almost doesn't want to know.

-You left your gun... I didn't know where else to turn.

-Bill, you have no idea the risk you've taken coming here. You could've irrevocably damaged the Tipler Cylinder...

-Meaning?

-Meaning you could be stuck here! And you're not prepared for life in this century.

-I can handle it. They say if you consume a certain amount of Yage you obtain godlike omnipotence...

-You're saying you're a god now?

-I'm a god but not in the monotheistic sense. I'm not a demiurge.

Kip dismisses Burroughs junk ravaged nonsense and retrieves the photonic crystal gun from the toilet seat. He inspects the barrel briefly then cocks it at the far wall of the bathroom. Kip squeezes the trigger and nothing happens.

-Yup, you've fucking broken it.

Burroughs scrambles to the window sill and pushes the glass frame open. He glares outside at the strange, alien infested metropolis of Glasgow.

-So this is Scotland eh?

-Last time I checked.

-What a place!

-I'm going to have to get my hands on another gun. Christ, this means I'm going to have to act all paly with Deacon Fairfax. Fuck sake Bill, d'you have any idea the hassle you're causing me?

Burroughs gives an ambivalent glance before returning to the view out the bathroom window.

-What are the rules about firearms in this fuckin' joint? It's not an anachronism of your time is it? It's the future, I guess that means you're all packin' heat huh?

-We're not gun nuts Bill, but having a weapon is cool if you got a license.

-I want one of your time-travelling guns, wow, what a kick!

-You're not a licensed TD.

Novikov becomes aware of a presence in the doorway—

it's Crystal. She's nursing a shotgun—Crystal's "occupation" was as a shotgun artist. She would inject paint capsules into a laser propelled shotgun and fire them at a canvas. The subsequent pieces sell for very little money but she is highly sought after in the creative community.

-Kip, why are there two naked old men in my bathroom?

Two naked old men?

Kip then notices a heavy breathing coming from behind the sink. The figure emerges nude, straightens his back and declares:

—You stole my fuckin' book...

Before Kip can process any of this, Crystal has collapsed onto the bathroom tiles. She's clutching her stomach beneath her nightgown. A green ooze has covered the floor from a source between her legs. She looks up at Kip accusingly.

-You fucked Night Slime???

AFTERWORD

One of the greatest benefits of living a literary life runs parallel to the adventures and advances a writer creates in the arena of his own career. It owes to discovering the work of other writers and following their journey, as experienced via characters, settings, and turns of phrases. Some of that allure surely is voyeuristic, a quality inherent in all scribes—we love those furtive glimpses of different, private lives we steal through our neighbors' windows. But at its heart is the pure joy of getting lost in another writer's vision, of turning pages hungry to know what happens next after we've been seduced.

Chris Kelso's superlative *The Folger Variation and Other Lies* is one such must-read book written by that caliber of writer. On a gloomy December Friday afternoon—our thirteenth consecutive day of gray skies in the outer limits of Northern New Hampshire where I live and write; nearby Mount Washington has a penchant for gathering and holding onto cloud cover—I wrapped work on longhand pages, deadlines, and work-related emails, and opened the file of Mister Kelso's latest effort, which I had agreed to review. Despite crossed eyes and depleted energy (my body sometimes forgets that it's not fifteen anymore, that it's spiraling closer to its fifth decade of life on Spaceship Earth, but is frequently reminded of this fact come twilight), I blinked and had reached the end of the story. A glance at the clock confirmed time had passed, and my cup of Darjeeling tea, heavy on milk and light on the sugar, sat empty. I hadn't merely turned the pages; I was transported into them, and believed in the realness of the world I'd visited.

Granted, *Folger* isn't the longest read, but so often less *is* more, and the author's tale of time travel, multiplicity, upper crust aliens from Ursa Minor, dead wives and damned toddlers, and a grandfather who wishes upon himself a robot son instead of his own flesh and blood, is as rewarding a read in its brevity as anything gargantuan penned by King or Tolstoy. The words are poetic, sumptuous; as beautiful as they are ugly in equal doses, which is another of Mister Kelso's strongest gifts.

I was already aware of the author's work through his original shared universe series, the Slave States. I'd had a similar experience with The Black Dog Eats the City, a standalone entry into Mister Kelso's franchise of other-dimensional, alien-controlled mining enclaves populated by nihilistic and forsaken unfortunates. Kelso states that he based the Slave State mythos upon his native soil, the landscape he inhabits and sees daily living outside Glasgow, the U.K.'s third-largest metropolis. *Dog*, too, drew me in like light spilling into a voracious singularity; escape was impossible—not that I wanted to leave any more than I did with *Folger* upon reaching *The End*.

Arthur Folger learns that it's impossible to escape one's history and identity. This voyeuristic reader and fan selfishly hopes the same holds true for Chris Kelso, who is telling engaging stories in a unique voice and may find that, like Dickens and Lovecraft long before him, an entire new style of fiction crops up to pay homage to his byline as a result.

I can't wait to read what future Kelsoian efforts are forthcoming.

Gregory L. Norris

Gregory L. Norris, Writer *Tales From the Robot Graveyard*, Screenwriter *Brutal Colors* (Feature Film)

CRITICAL PRAISE FOR CHRIS KELSO

Chris Kelso is a writer of almost intimidating intelligence, wit, and imagination. On every page there is evidence of a great mind at work. Just when you're wondering if there are actually still writers out there who still feel and live their ideas out on the page, I come across a writer like Kelso, and suddenly the future feels a lot more optimistic. One calls to mind Burroughs, and Trocchi's more verbose offerings-whilst remaining uniquely himself, in a writer as young as he is, is a very encouraging sign: one of maturity that belies his youth. I look forward to reading more from him in the near future.'

Andrew Raymond Drennan
author of *The Immaculate Heart*

Chris Kelso sets his photonic crystal gun on KILL and takes no prisoners. My favorite era of science fiction was the 60s "New Wave" when the British magazine NEW WORLDS took front and centre, and there's a bit of NEW WORLDS here, kind of like Jerry Cornelius using the cut-up method in a bungalow in Glasgow, with a splash of Warren Ellis added for extra flavour. Kelso has a compelling voice. Somewhere Papa Burroughs is smiling.

L. L. Soares
author of *Life Rage and In Sickness*

Chris Kelso is an important satirist, I think it's safe to say.

Anna Tambour
author of *Crandolin*

Someday soon people will be naming him as one of their own influences

INTERZONE magazine

Come into the dusty deserted publishing house where mummified editors sit over moth-eaten manuscripts of books that were never written...anyone who enjoys the work of my late friend William Burroughs will feel welcome here with Chris Kelso.'

Graham Masterton

Chris Kelso's prose swaggers like blues and jitters like bebop. Dig.

Nate Southard
author of *Down* and *Just Like Hell*

Sparky, modern, avant-garde but accessible, Chris Kelso's book is reminiscent of the most successful literary experimentation of the 60s and 70s, the sort of work that was published in the later New Worlds, but it's also thoroughly contemporary, intimately engaged with modern life as it is right now. Kelso steams with talent and dark wit and his blend of anarchy with precision is refreshing, inspiring and utterly entertaining . . .

Rhys Hughes
author of *Mister Gum*

This emerging journeyman of the macabre has wormed his way into my grey-matter and continues to seep noxious ichor. I feel like I must devour him. Every little bit of him.

Adam Lowe

Chris Kelso's writing is like a punch to the gut that forces your face against the page. The way his gritty prose carries his imagination is like a bar fight between Bradbury and Bukowski, with the reader coming out on top. The worlds he drags us into are so damn ugly that you have to admire their beauty.

Chris Boyle of BizarroCast

Whether he's writing about a fictionalized William Burroughs, Time Detectives, or Aliens Chris Kelso aims at the interstices or the Interzones because he understands that these are the people and spaces that define modern life—Kelso is also always funny and twisted.'

Douglas Lain

Choke down a handful of magic mushrooms and hop inside a rocket ship trip to futuristic settings filled with pop culture, strange creatures and all manner of sexual deviance.

Richard Thomas
author of *Transubstantiate*

Guaranteed to uplift the heart of today's most discerningly jaded nihilist.

Tom Bradley

Chris Kelso is the one your mother warned you about. He is a sick, sick man-bereft of cure and heaped with symptom. His words will taint you irrevocably. Your eyes will want to gargle after reading just one of his stories.

Steve Vernon
author of *Nothing to Lose*

.

Printed in Great Britain
by Amazon